MARÍA CELESTE ARRARÁS

The Magic Cane

ILLUSTRATED BY PABLO RAIMONDI

WITH COLOR BY CHRIS CHUCKRY

Orchard Books • New York • An Imprint of Scholastic Inc.

Once upon a time in a faraway kingdom, a mighty emperor ruled in peace and prosperity. He had a son named Moconoco and spoiled him so outrageously that Moconoco turned into a selfish and willful boy. The other children shunned him. His only friend was a peasant boy named Karmelo, who felt sorry for Moconoco.

One day, when the boys were playing in the forest, an old woman appeared before them, hobbling along, leaning heavily on a shining gold cane.

"Hello, my little ones. Welcome to my forest home," she said.

Karmelo bowed politely to the old woman, but Moconoco showed no such respect. He cared only about the gleaming cane, eyeing it greedily. "Give me your cane!" he demanded. "I am the Emperor's son and I command you!"

Karmelo, too, was fascinated by the golden cane but he was shocked by Moconoco's rude and unfair demand. "Leave her alone," said Karmelo. "She needs the cane to help her walk."

Moconoco just laughed. He grabbed the cane from the frail old woman, who stumbled and fell to the ground. The cane seemed to throb in Moconoco's hand. As he waved it in the air, sparks flew from the tip, and Moconoco felt a powerful shock shoot up his arm. Karmelo gasped in horror. Moconoco laughed again. "Don't worry, Karmelo," he said. "I'll share the cane three ways, one for each of us, if that makes you happy." And before Karmelo could stop him, Moconoco broke the gleaming cane into three pieces, which instantly faded from gold into plain wood.

From down on the ground, the old woman looked at Moconoco and proclaimed, "You have no sense of right or wrong. So from now on, you greedy boy, you will have three of all your other senses!"

Moconoco was delighted. What a fine reward! he thought.

Karmelo was confused by the old woman's words, but he could not take time to ponder them; he needed to help her.

He found a fallen branch from a tree and, helping her to her feet, said, "It's not as beautiful as your golden cane, but it will help you walk."

The old woman smiled at Karmelo. Then she picked up the three pieces of wood that had been the golden cane and handed them to the boy. "These hold the key to defeat evil. You will find happiness when the three become one again."

"Come!" said Moconoco impatiently. "She makes no sense. I break her cane and I get a reward. You try to help her and all you get are three useless pieces of wood!"

As Moconoco dragged Karmelo away, laughing merrily, the old woman smiled. "Laugh all you want, my little one," she said. "You will soon realize that today you received a curse, not a reward. More is not always better!" Then she disappeared into the forest.

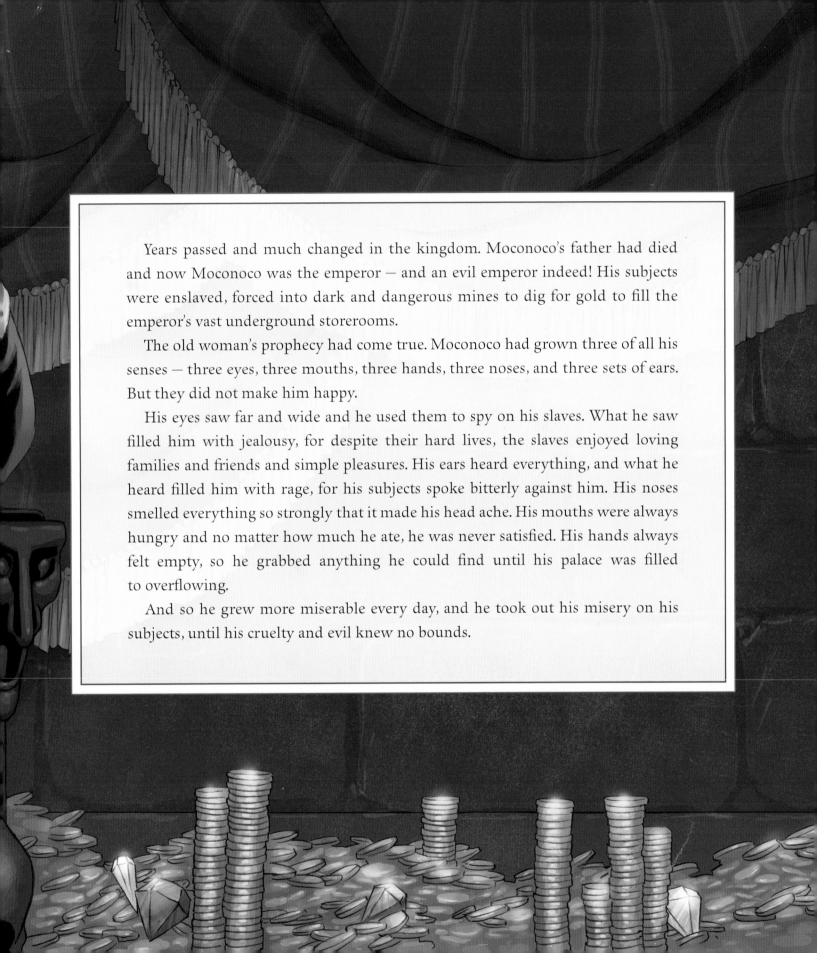

Years passed and much changed in the kingdom. Moconoco's father had died and now Moconoco was the emperor — and an evil emperor indeed! His subjects were enslaved, forced into dark and dangerous mines to dig for gold to fill the emperor's vast underground storerooms.

The old woman's prophecy had come true. Moconoco had grown three of all his senses — three eyes, three mouths, three hands, three noses, and three sets of ears. But they did not make him happy.

His eyes saw far and wide and he used them to spy on his slaves. What he saw filled him with jealousy, for despite their hard lives, the slaves enjoyed loving families and friends and simple pleasures. His ears heard everything, and what he heard filled him with rage, for his subjects spoke bitterly against him. His noses smelled everything so strongly that it made his head ache. His mouths were always hungry and no matter how much he ate, he was never satisfied. His hands always felt empty, so he grabbed anything he could find until his palace was filled to overflowing.

And so he grew more miserable every day, and he took out his misery on his subjects, until his cruelty and evil knew no bounds.

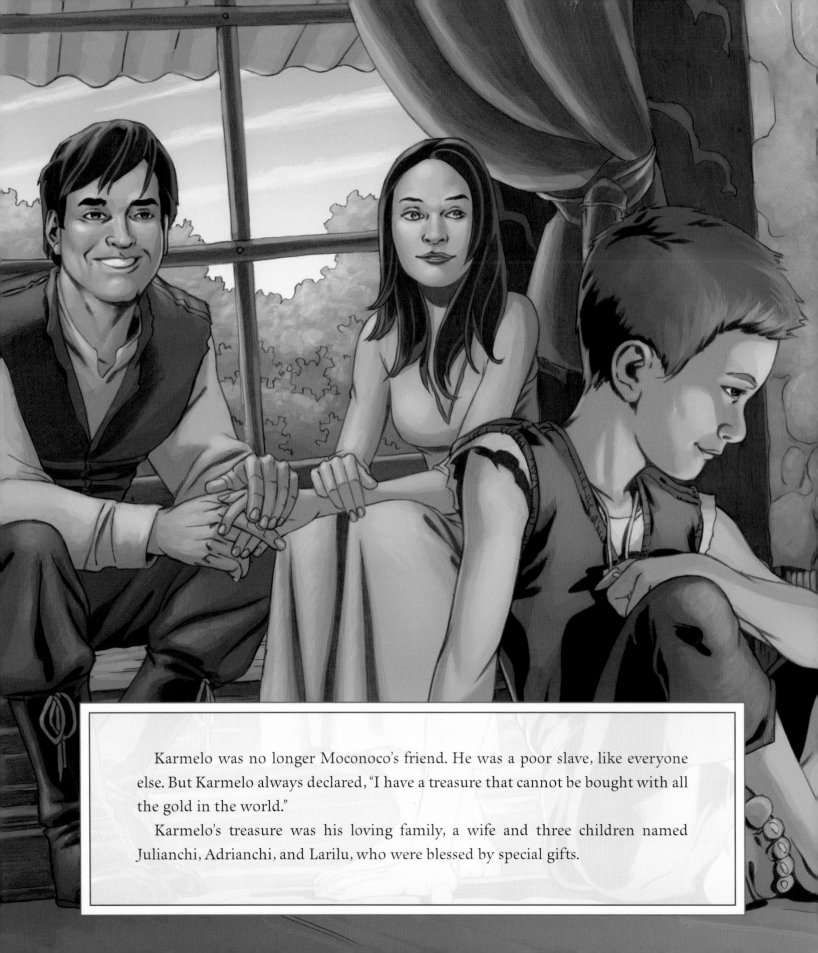

Karmelo was no longer Moconoco's friend. He was a poor slave, like everyone else. But Karmelo always declared, "I have a treasure that cannot be bought with all the gold in the world."

Karmelo's treasure was his loving family, a wife and three children named Julianchi, Adrianchi, and Larilu, who were blessed by special gifts.

When each child turned three, Karmelo gave them the only birthday present he could afford, one of the pieces of wood from the old woman's cane. And each time, something extraordinary happened. For a brief moment, the wood glittered like gold, sparks flew from its tip, and the child felt a powerful shock. Then the special gift was revealed.

Karmelo urged his children to use their gifts to help others. And as the years went by, all three children realized that the best way to help would be to get rid of the evil Moconoco and free the slaves. They each tried to defeat the emperor on their own.

The oldest child, Julianchi, had the gift of the wind. Julianchi blew up a powerful tornado and sent it spinning to toss the emperor off his throne. But Moconoco used his three arms to grab on to the throne and hold fast as the wind tore past him.

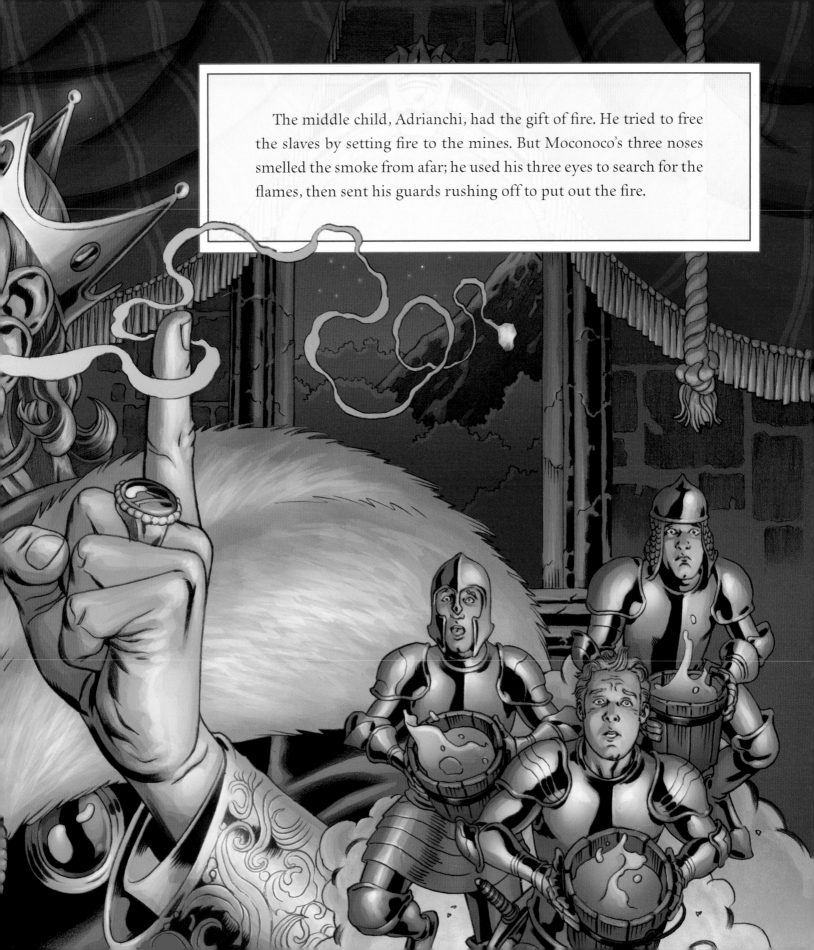

The middle child, Adrianchi, had the gift of fire. He tried to free the slaves by setting fire to the mines. But Moconoco's three noses smelled the smoke from afar; he used his three eyes to search for the flames, then sent his guards rushing off to put out the fire.

And the youngest child, Larilu, had the gift of water. She could spill forth tidal waves and churning rapids. Larilu sent a huge tidal wave down the river to try to drown the emperor while he was bathing. But Moconoco's three ears heard the roar of the rushing waters well before they reached him and he scurried to safety on the riverbank.

Moconoco felt very powerful. Having **three** of every sense is a blessing after all, he told himself. So he decided that his wrath would be **three** times greater than usual and he offered a reward **three** times larger than the largest ever given to anyone who could capture the children.

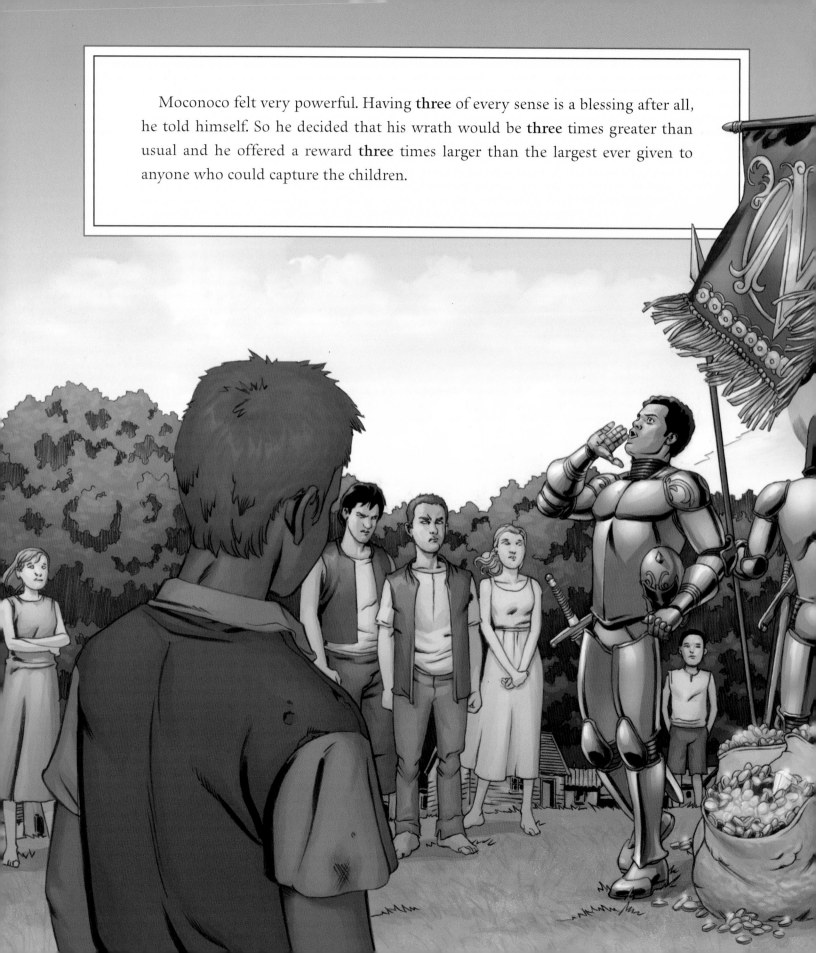

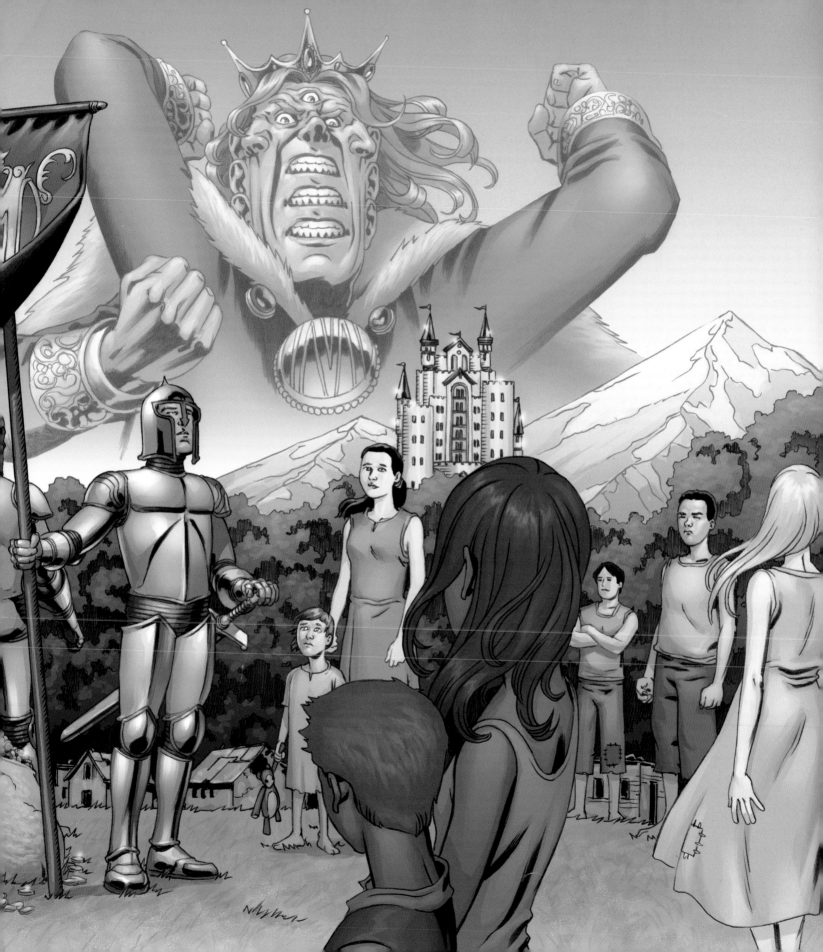

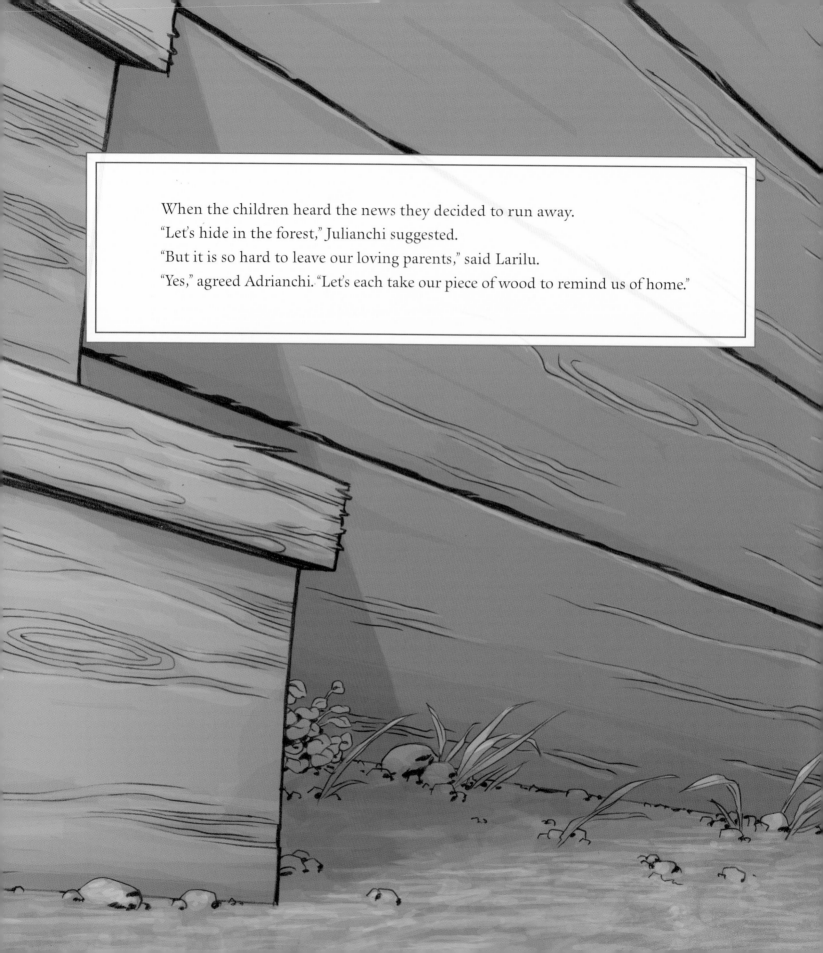

When the children heard the news they decided to run away.

"Let's hide in the forest," Julianchi suggested.

"But it is so hard to leave our loving parents," said Larilu.

"Yes," agreed Adrianchi. "Let's each take our piece of wood to remind us of home."

Karmelo and his wife were desperate. How could they try to protect their children, when they could not find them anywhere? Finally, Karmelo had an idea. "Perhaps they fled to the forest. It was a good place to hide when Moconoco and I were young."

And sure enough, that is where Karmelo found them, surviving on the fruits that Julianchi blew off the trees, on the fresh water that Larilu gave them to drink, and keeping warm by the fire Adrianchi made for them.

"My dear children," said Karmelo, pride and relief shining from his eyes, "how good it is to see you helping one another. This will give you strength."

But the happy reunion was soon over. Moconoco, leading his guards, had followed Karmelo and soon discovered the secret hiding place. He was delighted that he had found the children by himself so no reward would be paid. Happily, he called out, "You are surrounded. Surrender at once! You will be the first of many children to be forced to work in the mines!"

Karmelo was outraged. He would not let Moconoco abuse anyone ever again — especially not his beloved children! For the first time in many, many years, he remembered the old woman's words, and finally they made sense.

Picking up the three pieces of wood, he turned to his children. "These hold the key to defeat evil," he cried. Suddenly, the wood began to glow and the three pieces merged into one — the shining golden cane! The children stared in wonder and then the truth dawned on them. Only by fighting together could they defeat the evil emperor.

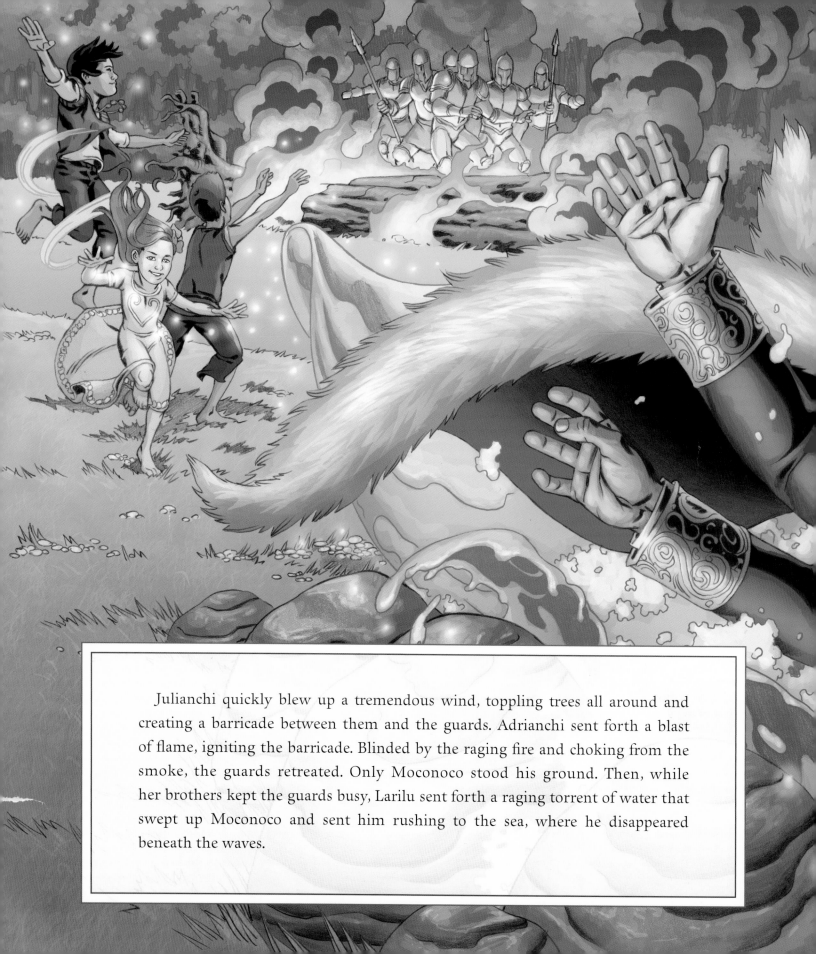

Julianchi quickly blew up a tremendous wind, toppling trees all around and creating a barricade between them and the guards. Adrianchi sent forth a blast of flame, igniting the barricade. Blinded by the raging fire and choking from the smoke, the guards retreated. Only Moconoco stood his ground. Then, while her brothers kept the guards busy, Larilu sent forth a raging torrent of water that swept up Moconoco and sent him rushing to the sea, where he disappeared beneath the waves.

The evil emperor was defeated! Peace and prosperity returned to the kingdom. Karmelo lived a long life, surrounded by his three beloved children, who from then on always joined together, using their gifts to help others. Karmelo had indeed found true happiness — just as the old woman had promised.

And, deep in the forest, the old woman smiled. "It was just a matter of time — as I knew it would be," she declared. "Evil is always punished and goodness rewarded." Then she disappeared among the trees once more.

For Julian, Adrian, and Lara, who have the power of love
and showed me that 3 is a magical number...
m.c.A.

For Ana and Carlos, my mom and dad, always my greatest
supporters.

p.R.

Copyright © 2007 by María Celeste Arrarás

Illustrations copyright © 2007 by Pablo Raimondi

Coloring by Chris Chuckry

Library of Congress Cataloging-in-Publication Data

Arrarás, María Celeste.

The magic cane / by María Celeste Arrarás ; illustrated by Pablo Raimondi. — 1st ed. p. cm.
Summary: A prophecy and a broken cane given to him in his childhood help a simple peasant and his
children, who have power over wind, fire, and water, to defeat a wicked emperor who was once the
peasant's friend. ISBN-13: 978-0-439-57419-8 ISBN-10: 0-439-57419-6 (reinforced lib. bdg.) [1. Conduct of life —
Fiction. 2. Family life — Fiction. 3. Cooperativeness — Fiction. 4. Fairy tales.] I. Raimondi, Pablo, ill. II. Title.

PZ8.A883Mag 2007   [E]—dc22 2006030365

10 9 8 7 6 5 4 3 2 1   07 08 09 10 11   Printed in Singapore 46

First edition, October 2007